E.T.
THE EXTRA-TERRESTRIAL

A FRIEND FOR E.T.

adapted by Gail Herman
based on a motion-picture screenplay by Melissa Mathison

Simon Spotlight
New York London Toronto Sydney Singapore

SIMON SPOTLIGHT

An imprint of Simon & Schuster Children's Publishing Division
1230 Avenue of the Americas, New York, New York 10020
Copyright © 2002 Universal Studios Publishing Rights, a division
of Universal Studios Licensing, Inc. *E.T. The Extra-Terrestrial* is
a trademark and copyright of Universal Studios.
Manufactured in the United States of America
First Edition 10 9 8 7 6 5 4 3 2 1
ISBN 0-689-84363-1

It was a cool, starlit night. A spaceship hovered above a redwood forest, then slowly landed in a clearing. The hatch slid open and E.T. walked carefully down a ramp. Then he took his first step onto Earth.

E.T. stared at the giant trees as his friends followed quietly behind.

So this was Earth, the planet where they'd come to look for plants.

An owl hooted. E.T. jumped. What kind of creatures lived in this strange place?

E.T. could see rows of yellow lights past the forest. Curious, he edged away from the woods, toward the lights. But E.T. made sure he could still see the spaceship. He didn't want to wander *too* far.

Roar!
Suddenly a car
thundered past.

Headlights lit the darkness
and E.T. threw himself to the
ground. He rolled down a
hill, away from his spaceship
. . . away from his friends.

More cars screeched to a
stop. Shouts broke the quiet
of the forest, and more lights
flashed all around. E.T.
ducked behind some low
branches and peeked out.

Earth creatures! E.T. thought.
They were searching for something.

One of E.T.'s friends stood at the hatch of the spaceship waiting for him.

The **red light** in his friend's chest flashed. He's signaling! E.T. thought.

The Earth creatures spotted E.T. and chased him through the tall grass. He had to get back to his spaceship! His heart beat furiously, and a red light glowed within his chest.

Then E.T. saw another red flash and the hatch closed. His friends were leaving! And now he was all alone on this planet.

How was he going to get home?

Sadly, E.T. waddled from tree to tree, heading toward the houses by the forest. Finally he stopped in front of a house with a vegetable garden, an orange tree, and a glowing red light on a post.

Comforted by the plants and the light, E.T. bravely found a hiding place inside a toolshed behind the house.

Suddenly a voice called out, "Harvey? Are you in there?" E.T. froze.

"Here, boy!" A ball rolled into the shed, right by E.T.! After a moment E.T. picked it up and rolled it back.

"Aaaahh!" screamed the voice. "There's something in the toolshed!"

Soon there were more voices. An Earth creature stepped into the toolshed and flashed a light. E.T. held his breath.

"There's nothing in here," the creature said, going back outside.

"Wait!" someone else said. "Look at these strange footprints."

"The coyote came back," said another voice. Then E.T. heard footsteps going away from the toolshed.

When it was quiet E.T. stepped out of the shed. He was curious. He wandered around the garden and found himself among some cornstalks.

Suddenly the cornstalks parted and a light flashed in E.T.'s eyes. It was a small Earth creature!

E.T. screamed. The creature flung himself to the ground.

I must escape! E.T. thought as he scurried around the creature.

But the creature lifted his head. **"Don't go,"** he whispered.

E.T. hurried away, rushing as fast as he could back to the forest. Maybe the spaceship had come back. Maybe his friends were there waiting for him in the clearing.

But by the next morning the spaceship still wasn't there. What if the Earth creatures came back? Where could he go?

Then he looked down, and spotted a small, round candy . . . and another . . . and another. It was a trail!

E.T. followed the colorful candy pieces. They seemed to lead back to the houses. E.T. walked slowly, careful to stay hidden, picking up the candy pieces as he went. And then he saw the last candy—right by the same house he was at the night before.
E.T. hid behind
a bush and
waited.

That night E.T. peeked out from his hiding place.
He saw the small Earth creature sleeping in the backyard.
E.T. edged closer. He looked at the creature.

Just then the creature opened his eyes. He looked
scared as he stared at E.T.

E.T. was not scared. He came closer to the creature.
Slowly, so the creature wouldn't be scared, E.T. stretched
out his arm, opened his hand, and dropped a handful of
candy pieces onto the creature's lap.

The creature smiled. He dug into his pocket and started a new trail of candy pieces into his house. E.T. followed close behind.

E.T. followed the creature up the stairs and into a room. In the room were so many things E.T. had never seen before.

The creature touched his eye. E.T. touched his own eye. The boy touched his mouth. E.T. touched his own mouth.

E.T. wanted to talk to the creature, but he felt so tired he could only yawn. The creature placed a blanket on him. And E.T. fell asleep.

The next morning the creature asked E.T., "Do you talk?"
E.T. was silent.

"Me human. Boy," the creature said.
"Elliott. Ell-ee-ut."

Still, E.T. said nothing.

"Well, maybe you're hungry,"

Elliott said. He made sandwiches, then showed E.T. around his bedroom and the bathroom. He filled the tub for E.T. to take a bath and E.T. sighed. The boy was nice.

E.T. watched Elliott move things in his closet, making a big empty space. Then he placed a blanket on the floor, along with pillows, water, and a bag of cookies.

"This is your home," Elliott told E.T. "You stay. Okay? I'll be right here with you."

E.T. nodded.

E.T. stayed in the closet, surrounded by toys and stuffed animals.

Elliott, he thought to himself. **Elliott was his friend.** And he was sure Elliott would help him find his way back to his real home.